I0673611

Leonard Swett

Remembrances of T. Lyle Dickey

Leonard Swett

Remembrances of T. Lyle Dickey

ISBN/EAN: 9783337815622

Printed in Europe, USA, Canada, Australia, Japan

Cover: Foto ©Andreas Hilbeck / pixelio.de

More available books at **www.hansebooks.com**

REMEMBRANCES

—(OF)—

T. LYLE DICKEY,

—(BY)—

LEONARD SWETT.

———▶———

BARNARD & GUNTHORP, PRINTERS.

UNITED STATES CIRCUIT COURT,

NORTHERN DISTRICT OF ILLINOIS.

MAY IT PLEASE THE COURT:

> "Take heed that in thy verse,
> Thou dost the tale rehearse,
> Else dread a dead man's curse;
> For this I sought thee."

Mr. Longfellow, our greatest poet, being at Newport, Rhode Island, and seeing there the old round tower,— that work of unknown date, of unknown architecture, and of unknown nationality,—and hearing also that a skeleton had been recently found at Fall River, near by, spun out that beautiful romance, "The Skeleton in Armor," in which he makes the tower the architecture of Norwegians in the twelfth century and the skeleton that of an old viking or corsair of the same period, who built the house for his home, after stealing his wife and crossing the ocean, and when she died buried her under the tower, and, overwhelmed with grief at her loss and crying out, "Never shall the sun rise on such another," fell full-armed upon his spear and lay there covered with the sands of time until his body thus encased in corroded armor was found about the time Mr. Longfellow was there.

The lines of this *true* story with which I begin this

talk are what the skeleton said to the poet, enjoining upon him the duty of telling this dead man's tale.

These lines have rung in my mind many an hundred times during the last two years, and the following is the history of their haunting me:

Once, and only once, since I have had my offices in the Montauk block, some five years, Judge Dickey came up there to see me. He being fourteen years my senior, I used to visit him. He came up to the eighth story, having apparently walked up some of the flights of stairs and was considerably out of breath when he came in. "Swett," said he, "as I was walking along the sidewalk below, I was thinking of you, and have come up to see you." I replied: "I am very glad to see you, judge, as I always am." " But I came of a special errand, and to see if you would promise to do something for me." I replied: " It will give me great pleasure to promise or do anything you could ask of me." He replied: "Well, I have come up to ask you when I die to say something in commemoration of my character. I believe you can appreciate and call out, better than any other person I know, any points of my character worthy to be remembered, and I have come in all seriousness to make this request." I replied, " Judge, I will make the promise to you if you will make the same to me if I die first." He said, "I will," and rose and offered me his hand across the table, which I accepted, and there, alone, we confirmed to each other these promises.

Within a few days after this Judge Dickey had a terrible fall, by stepping back off the stage at Apollo hall in this city, and I thought he had come to me by prophetic instinct, and that his time had come, but he recovered and died about two years ago.

It looks like a late day now for the fulfillment of this promise, but "better late than never." When Judge Dickey died I was myself sick in Maine, and I did not regain my health until last September, and since then my duties to the living, also badly neglected, have pressed upon me, and this occasion is the first time I have caught up with this duty. But I have not been day by day, in my neglect, without a gentle reminder, for these lines of Mr. Longfellow with which I commenced have, morning, noon and night, been constantly ringing in my head, until goaded by them I am here, like Jonah, for the fulfillment of this neglected duty.

I find, on looking the matter over, that at the time of the death of Judge Dickey, the bar of this city held a meeting and adopted a memorial, and among its appointments named me as the one who should present this memorial to this court. I have that memorial now, and present it, and respectfully ask that your Honor may order it to be spread upon the records of this court It is in the usual form, and justly commendatory of one of the bright lights of our profession.

I first met Judge Dickey about thirty-five years ago in the autumn of 1852. He was then judge of the circuit, and was holding court at Princeton, in Bureau county. I entered the court-house, and was introduced to him while he was sitting upon the bench. He was just then about to retire from the judgeship, and, asking me to be seated, the ceremony of his retiring and his successor assuming the duties of his position began. When they were completed and the new judge had taken his seat, Judge Dickey came down from the bench, took my arm, and we walked to the front of the court-house. There, standing on the steps and looking at the

green sward of the court-yard, he said aloud to everybody: " Now that I have laid aside the dignity of a
judge, I will make a wager that I can jump farther on
this green grass than any man in Bureau county."

· This anecdote illustrates one of the elements of his
character—his adaptability to everybody, his overflowing good humor, and his kind and genial social nature.
He met every one with a cheerful and sincere smile.
His normal condition was: " Peace on earth and good
will to men." He was affable, kind, courteous, and
polite, and made every one feel at ease in his presence.
I never knew him, in more than thirty years of intimate
acquaintance, to be guilty of a trick, or to be sharp or
deceitful, and never heard him accused of these faults
of character by any one. He was an open-hearted, kind,
manly, but skillful and wise man. It was, however, as
a trial lawyer in the circuit court that Judge Dickey
pre-eminently excelled and appeared most con-
spicuously and to advantage. Here he was always at
his best. Memory recalls him now, standing in a
court-room, half way through a long and complicated
trial, a pleasant smile upon his face, in the best of
humor, and fully equal to the situation. Here he was
gentlemanly, overflowing with good nature, quick,
sharp, and incisive as a Damascus blade. Playing with
him under such circumstances was like playing with
broken glass. Such moments with him were moments
of supreme coolness and supreme good nature. He
was thoroughly master of his place, smiling, happy,
quick as a cat. When Dickey stood in a court-room
and smiled and twirled the fob of his watch-chain,
look out! It is conceded that Judge Logan, of Spring-
field, was, for quickness and strength, the best trial

lawyer this state has ever produced. Judge Dickey was more like him than any man I ever knew. If I had a long, tangled controversy in court and could have two associates, I would rather have Judge Dickey in his prime for one than any man living.

He always had a new sight of every complication, and hence he was also most valuable as a counselor. Any man who spends his life dealing with tangled skeins knows well, after he has looked over a subject, as he thinks, in every possible light, and calls in some men as additional counsel, how such counsel too often will tramp over the same ground as has tramped over, and how he gets simply the old light he has always had, and how, when he goes to some other men and shows them his skein all tangled, a single remark made throws a new light on the whole subject, and how he gets a new view of the situation. Judge Dickey had always this new light and communicated this new view. He had an original, peculiar conception, personal to himself, and I never went to him for advice on any subject that I did not get some new light.

Judge Dickey was a man of unusually clear intellectual sight. He was wholly unlike a man whose vision was dimmed, and who as he looks out upon a landscape sees rocks and trees and landscape confused; he saw everything distinctly, and was wise and accurate in his perceptions and conduct. An anecdote of thirty years ago illustrates this, and may be useful to young men in the profession, and to old men; too. I was then about thirty-two years old. Dickey was forty-six, or in the prime of his professional experince. It had been seven years since I could call myself a lawyer in name, and I was defending the notorious Isaac Wyant, who had had an arm shot off in a fight, and who six months afterward walked into the court house at Clinton and shot four bullets through the man who had shot him. It was my first case of this kind. The trial lasted a week of long days and evenings, and the defendant was prosecuted by Abraham Lincoln. I had had the case in hand about a year and a half, and the facts and law of it were thoroughly tanned into me. I had been to Boston to consult Dr. Luther V. Bell, the great expert in insanity. I had also consulted Dickey, and he had promised if he could he would assist me at the trial; but, when the trial day came, my principal witness stampeded and wanted to go home, and Dickey was accidentally at the McLean court; and I was about scared to death. I fell on Dickey with his old promise that he would help me, but he declined. I offered him all the fee I was to get, but still not only he would not and went home, but he would give me no reason why he would not, and so I had "to tread the wine-press alone."

Afterward meeting Dickey, I said: " Now please tell me why you wouldn't help me?" He replied: " Because I could see you needed to be thrown on your own resources, and if I had been there you would have leaned on me, would have lost your own efficiency, and I was not familiar enough with the case to do the work well. No, when a young man is well prepared he should not undertake to filter his knowledge to the jury through an older man who is not prepared."

" Well," I replied, " why didn't you give me that reason?"

" Because you were strained then, and in a very useful state of distress, and if I had given you that reason I was afraid you would have beaten me out of it, and so I thought I would wait and tell you afterward."

Judge Dickey married and taught school in Ohio before he was twenty-one. Subsequently he took his wife to Kentucky and attempted to get a school there. He proposed to begin if twelve scholars could be assured him at four dollars each. This was more than the people were accustomed to pay, and finally, with twelve scholars at three dollars each, he began. Among these he found a rude, bad boy, and after bearing with him awhile, Dickey sent him home with a note to his father asking him to take him out of school. The father came with the boy the next morning, telling Dickey to take him back and to whip him. This he declined to do. He said his contract was to teach the boy and not to whip him. Finally Dickey agreed he would whip the boy, for the father, if he wanted it done and would stand there and superintend the work. The boy was sent for the switch and the father stood by and saw this whipping, at his request. The next day Dickey sent a bill to the father, about as follows:

To T. Lyle Dickey, Dr.
To whipping your boy at your request.........$3.00

The father grumbled, but finally paid the bill. The fame of this caused Dickey to be known as the schoolmaster who charged extra for whipping, and immediately his school filled to overflowing.

Judge Dickey moved from Kentucky to Illinois before the panic of 1837. He brought a sum of money which he had accumulated there and invested it in Illinois, lost it all, and became crippled with debt, which he carried for a life-time. About this time he made the acquaintance of Cyrus Walker, an eminent lawyer of those days.

Mr. Walker persuaded him to commence the study of law and put out his shingle at the same time. As clients came, he would take the facts of the case, walk seven miles to where Mr. Walker lived, and get posted. Mr. Cyrus Walker used to assist Dickey at this time to family necessaries, and it is, in fact, to him that we are indebted for Judge Dickey, as one of the good works Mr. Walker left.

When the bankrupt law of 1841 was passed, a question of right and wrong was presented to Judge Dickey in reference to his old indebtedness. If there was ever a case in which a man was justified in taking the benefit of a bankrupt law, Dickey was, because there was no question but that the debt arose from misfortune, and he had nothing. The law was made for just such a case, but such a course did not accord with Dickey's conscientious notions of integrity, and he carried along the debt, paying as he could, until 1867, when the last of it, with interest, was finally liquidated. Thus he held it to be conscientious in himself, and a duty to pay the " uttermost farthing," although it took him thirty years, the best of his life, to do it.

And not only did he do this, but temptation came to him in this matter double-edged. About 1842, when everybody else was taking the benefit of the bankrupt act, Dickey inherited some seven or eight slaves, left to him by a relative in Kentucky. It would have been very convenient to have sold these to relieve him from debt, but this too he conscientiously declined, and freed all his slaves.

Another peculiarity of his was, when he was a judge, and wanted advice as to how to decide a case, his habit was to consult children, and thus considered in connec-

tion with the case in hand their original but sharp
notions of right and wrong. He would state his case
to them in an understandable way, and say: "Now,
what should this man or that man be required to do?"
In this way he got to the very root of things, and to
original but simple and direct justice.

He entered the service in the war of the rebellion in
the spring of 1861. His name had been before Gover-
nor Yates for a colonel's appointment, but there was
some hitch about it, and he came to Bloomington,
where Judge Davis and I lived, from Ottawa, where he
lived, to consult with us as to how he could get into the
service of his country. Besides himself, he had sons
and sons-in-law and friends in La Salle county, who
also wanted to get in, but couldn't. We told him the
region of Bloomington was also full of men who wanted
to do the same thing, but couldn't. This was an unusual
thing in the history of patriotism in any country, but is
a fact of those times that the country was full of men
who wanted to serve it, but they could not get the
chance. It was finally determined that Dickey and
I should both go to Washington. We both knew Mr.
Lincoln, and I knew General Cameron, Secretary of
War, and he for past favors was indebted to Judge Davis
and myself. The object of this mission was to get
into the service these people in the various capacities
they were fitted to fill, in La Salle and McLean counties.
I was the more ready for this mission, because I had
made up my mind not to go into the service personally,
because I had a sick wife and a sick son wholly depend-
ent upon me for care, and if I left them nobody was to
take care of them. Besides, I had in my life been to
one war, and that, too, as a private soldier. So I made

up my mind that I would not go, but that I would serve every regiment and every man who did go. I could be absent from home in snatches of time. I need not add, as this became known I had plenty of business.

At Washington we got authority for Dickey to raise a regiment, which was done mainly in LaSalle and McLean counties, and appoint all the officers of it. He appointed William McCullough, of Bloomington, as lieutenant-colonel. He was the most thoroughly courageous man I have ever known, and entered the service at the age of fifty, with one arm and one eye. Afterwards he fell in a hopeless charge, at the head of his regiment, in Mississippi. We also obtained an order for 1,000 cavalry uniforms and 1,000 sabers and accoutrements and 1,000 Sharp carbines, to be sent directly from the manufactories to Ottawa. We were afraid if they were sent to Washington they would be needed by other regiments and we would not get them, and so we got this order directly on the factories for the first made. The regiment was soon and easily raised, but it was in the summer and quite late, and the uniforms, sabers, carbines, etc, had not come. They had a thousand men in camp at Ottawa and had written letters without number, and telegraphed until they had nearly burned the wires off, but no uniforms, accoutrements or carbines came. The men had become uneasy waiting about camp in farmer's clothes, and something had to be done.

It was finally decided by the officers in council to send me to Washington to see why these things did not come. I had already been there two or three times for them, and Dickey and his officers knew I didn't want to go again. I was then at the Danville court and Dickey came down there, about 150 miles, coming in the night, and about 4 o'clock in the morning I heard him pounding at my door at the hotel. I give you the interview as illustrative of his appropriateness, in saying always just the right thing to move a man and to effect his own purpose. "I know it was mean," he began, as he entered my room, I lying in bed. "I know it was mean, but in old Kentucky times, when we used to drive a six-horse team and were near miring down in a slough, we used to lick the best horse. It was awfully mean, but it was simply a necessity to get out of the mire, and that is what I have come clear from Ottawa to-night to do to you. I want you to get out of that bed and leave the court and go immediately to Washington and find out what has happened to our orders for clothing and arms. I can not leave my regiment. They are all in camp in farmer's clothes, and you can not drill a farmer boy to become a soldier until you put a new uniform on him, and give him a new sword and bright carbine. You know all about this business at Washington, and can get it done, and Col. McCullough and I have held a council of war and we have concluded you must go." What was left for me but to get up and start for Washington?

I will not, in a long time, forget my interview with Mr. Lincoln on this subject, and herein I want to correct a popular error in reference to the beginning of the war. Everybody says: "Pshaw! what made Lincoln call for 75,000 men? Why didn't he call for 500,000 at once?" I will tell you. The government did not call for 500,000 men, simply because it could not utilize them. The time of which I speak was the spring and summer of 1861.

The arming of the nation had been in progress for about four months. At the beginning the government had no arms. They had all been transported south. Europe had no surplus of good arms it could sell. All we could buy were mainly old Austrian muskets, the refuse of Austria, and they were good for nothing but to teach men to drill.

I learned when I arrived at Washington that the government in a pinch had ordered all the arms it could lay its hands on to Washington, to arm regiments there, and this order had been held to supersede our order. Mr. Lincoln, in not the best of humor, said: "Swett, if your regiment were to wait and take an honest turn, the wool has not yet grown on the sheep's back to make their uniforms." This is the key to the explanation why the government did not take men faster. It is also a reason which could not then be publicly told, for it would have shown to foreign nations our weakness. The industries of the nation had all to be changed. All the wool on the sheeps' backs in the country, and all that could be bought, had to be diverted to uniforms, and the manufacturing capacity of the country had to be increased, and Mr. Lincoln might have added with equal truth that the ore with which to make the swords and the carbines was still in its native mountains. All the manufactories in the country had to be set in operation to make arms. New factories had to be built and new industries created, and even then whole regiments had to wait for their turn to be uniformed and armed.

I said to Gov. Seward once: "Why did you in the beginning talk of peace in ninety days? Didn't you know we wouldn't have peace?"

"Yes;" he replied, "but it wouldn't do to say it, because of the fear of foreign intervention. We had better wait on this assertion three months, and then invent something else for the next three months."

Judge Dickey and his sons and sons-in-law have rendered marked services to their country, and deserve a monument more enduring than brass. They deserve the warm thanks of their countrymen, for whom they made these sacrifices. Let me recount the history of these two families, and let us pause and think whether their services and sacrifices do not equal the Fabii or the Gracchi or any other family of antiquity.

THEOPHILUS LYLE DICKEY left Ottawa for the Mexican war in 1846 as a captain of Company I, which became a part of Col. John J. Hardin's regiment. At San Antonio his regiment left him behind in camp to die of disease, but after hanging in the balance for a long time between life and death, he finally recovered.

GEN. WILLIAM H. L. WALLACE, Col. Dickey's son-in-law, had been a student in Dickey's law office, was the first lieutenant of Capt. Dickey's company, and afterward was made adjutant, and was at Col. Hardin's side when he fell at the battle of Buena Vista. He entered the service again in April, 1861, as colonel of the 11th infantry, was made a brigadier-general, and fell at Shiloh while endeavoring to stay the retreat of our army on Sunday, the first day of that terrible fight.

CYRUS C. DICKEY, Col. Dickey's oldest son, entered the service at the same time Col. Wallace did, and as a private in his regiment. Col. Ransom, a very young man, was a lover of battle for its own sake. His bright face seems to pass before me now. He was the son of the old veteran Ransom, who fell at Chepultepec. He became colonel of the 11th after Col. Wallace's promotion, and Cyrus Dickey was made adjutant upon his staff, and finally fell in Banks' expedition up the Red river, at Mansfield, Louisiana.

CHARLES H. DICKEY, the youngest son of Judge Dickey, entered the service with his father as a private in the 4th cavalry in July, 1861. He was made first-lieutenant, and was severely wounded while commanding Gen. McPherson's body-guard in the State of Mississippi. He is now a merchant in the Sandwich islands.

M. R. M. WALLACE, the brother of Col. Wallace, entered the service in the summer of 1861 as a major in the 4th cavalry with Col. Dickey, and was promoted for gallant service to the positions of colonel and brigadier-general. He was formerly the Probate judge of this county, and is now a practicing lawyer in this city.

JOHN F. WALLACE, another brother of Gen. Wallace, entered the service as lieutenant in Company C, with Col. Dickey, in the 4th cavalry, served gallantly through the war, was consolidated with Gen. Custer's 12th in the last part of the war in Texas, practiced law in Texas after the war, and died there. In a letter received from Mrs. Gen. Wallace, that lady, in speaking of him, says: " I always felt that he, too, was a victim of the war."

MATTHEW WALLACE, another brother, a farmer, entered the fourth cavalry in the summer of 1861, and in February, 1862, while embarking on a steamer with the troops at Cairo in a sleet storm to move up the Ohio, the guard-rail of the boat, on which he was leaning, broke, and he was plunged into the water with his carbine in hand, with his knapsack, haversack and saber strapped upon him, and a cavalry overcoat and boots on, and, although a splendid swimmer, sank beneath his load and was drowned.

C. H. WALLACE, who married Belle Dickey, Col.
Dickey's youngest daughter, another brother, also
served in the quartermaster's department under Col.
Fort. He was broken in health by his service and by
the small-pox which he contracted, and has never since
fully recovered. He is also now a merchant in the
Sandwich islands with Charles Dickey. Thus Col.
Dickey, with all his sons but one, and Col. William H.
L. Wallace, his son-in-law, with all his brothers, entered
the service of their country in the war of the rebellion,
and the seven were together at Shiloh.

MRS. GENERAL W. H. L. WALLACE, who was Judge
Dickey's eldest daughter, as the battle of Shiloh ap-
proached, became impressed with the sense of impend-
ing danger to her husband, then with Grant's army.
This impression haunted her until she could stand it
no longer, and in one of the most severe storms of the
season, at twelve o'clock at night, she started alone for
the army where her family were. At Cairo she was told
that no woman could be permitted to go up the Tennessee river. But affection has a persistency which will
not be denied. Mrs. Wallace finding a party bearing a
flag to the 11th infantry, from the ladies of Ottawa to
be used instead of theirs, which had been riddled and
was battle-worn, got herself substituted to carry that
flag, and thus with one expedient and another she finally
reached Shiloh, six hundred miles from home and three
hundred through a hostile country and through the
more hostile guards of our own forces.

She arrived on Sunday, the 6th of April, 1862, when
the great storm center of that battle was at its height,
and in time to receive her husband as he was borne
from the battle-field terribly mangled by a shot in the

head, which entered the eye and passed inside the skull and came out a little back of the ear, and which he had received while endeavoring to stay the retreat of our army as it was falling back to the banks of the river on that memorable Sunday, the first day of that bloody battle. She arrived in time to recognize him and be recognized by him, and a few days afterward, saying " We shall meet again in heaven," he died in the arms of that devoted wife, surrounded by Judge Dickey and his sons and the brothers of Gen. Wallace, and, as I am informed, in the very room then occupied by your honor as commander of the post at Savannah.

The story of the tragic death of Gen. Wallace and the circumstances of his wife's coming was told me by Judge Dickey on the battle-field of Shiloh, about Thursday or Friday of the same week.

It was through one of the accidents which so often changes the fate of battle, and which made Frederick the Great say battles were fought beyond the stars, that we are indebted to Col. Dickey more than any other man for the fact that the rebels did not effectually break through our lines at Fort Donelson and escape. Fort Donelson was on an ox-bow or sharp bend of the Tennessee river. The object of placing the fortification there was to command the river, and this position gave a shot nearly lengthwise down the river. Grant's maxim was to fight first and get ready as soon as he could, and thus have the selection of where the fight should be. His attack upon Donelson was made before his whole force arrived, and his tactics were to extend his line back of the fort from river to river, and thus hold the enemy in a *cul de sac*. To do this he had to stretch his lines like a piece of rubber—too far and make them too thin.

The object of the enemy when this line was extended and the fort could not be held was to break through and escape; so; finding the weakest point near the river, they bent back our lines as a wrestler bends back and dislocates the arm of his adversary, and began to pour through this opening, but finally voluntarily went back within the fortifications. These facts are well known, but the reason that induced the rebels to fight their way out and then voluntarily go back has not been known until since the war. and since the officers upon opposite sides have had an opportunity to compare notes.

Dickey had come to our lines at the fort, but his cavalry was unfit for such siege work, and there was no food for the horses there, so he was ordered back to a ridge and where he could get forage. This happened to be along the line of the road over which the remainder of Grant's army was expected by Grant and the rebels. As the soldiers pent up in the fort poured through our lines at the broken place and had proceeded a little way, they struck Dickey's force, which was about eighteen hundred men with some howitzers. Dickey immediately caused all his bugles to be blown and beat the long roll, and fired his howitzers sharply in the face of the enemy. They hesitated, stopped and went back into the fort, and thus Grant was enabled, finally, to report the capture of fourteen thousand men with the fortifications.

This attack was wholly unexpected, and it has since the war been learned from rebel officers who were there, that they did not expect to meet any force, and that they hesitated, stopped and turned back, their exit from the fort being in process of completion, because they supposed they had encountered the remainder of Grant's army and retreated, fearing they would be caught between this force coming and Grant's main force.

In all that adorns a man Judge Dickey was as bright as a new blade. He was quick and bright in his standard of honor. His professional and judicial character was pure and was never even sullied by suspicion or accusation. He occupied the public position of circuit judge in this state way back in the '50's, was a captain in the Mexican war, the colonel of 4th Illinois cavalry, brigadier general, and Gen. Grant's chief of the cavalry in the west. After the war he became assistant attorney-general of the United States, and finally was for many years one of the justices of our Supreme court of this state. In all these instances of holding official position he discharged the duties to the satisfaction of every one whose interests were affected, and the place he filled was honored by the fact that he filled it. The great charm and sweetness of his life, however, was an agreeable companion and friend. He was one of the few who were agreeable to sit down half a day with and to hear him talk. He was warm in love as a woman. In fact, Dickey was my first love. There are some marked advantages in loving a man. If a man loves a woman he must love but one, but in loving men numbers are not objectionable. I need not amplify. We all know how this is. I had known Dickey intimately for many years, had talked with him, had been on confidential relations with him from the first, and always loved him with a peculiar and marked affection.

One morning, as I went to my office at Bloomington, I met Dickey at the door. He had come down from

Ottawa on a night train which arrived about daylight, and was standing at my office door awaiting admission. Said he; "Where is Davis?" I told him, and he replied he wished I would send for him. When the judge came into my private office, Dickey said: "Gentlemen, we have been friends a great while; we have thought alike and acted alike; now I am going to leave you, and so I have come down to spend the day with you and bid you good-by. *I am going to join the democratic party.* I have not come to discuss whether I shall join it. In reference to that my mind is made up; but I thought, considering our past relations, it but fair, before leaving you, that I should come down and spend the day with you and bid you good-by. Then I shall go."

We had been old Henry Clay whigs together, and no men ever thought so exactly alike as Henry Clay whigs. The formation of the republican party was an element of disruption. Dickey had been raised in Kentucky, had a holy fear of abolition tendencies, although, as stated, he abolished his own slaves, and a tendency himself toward the democratic party, and by and by he determined to plunge in and join it.

We gave him a cordial welcome, went by ourselves, and gave up all business to the visit of the day. At noon we had a dinner together with a little Catawba, best the town afforded, and talked the day away. Politics, in fact, was the only subject absolutely avoided, for all the ground there had in many an interview been tramped over before. We talked over the olden times, told stories of circuit life, recalled those who had gone before, and when 4 o'clock in the afternoon, the time for Dickey to leave, came, we went with him to the train, shook him by the hand, bade him good-by. He did not stop until he ran into the very heart of the democratic party.

But old age let fall his mantle on the dear old judge, as it will let fall that mantle on us all. The pinched look and the feeble tread were finally his, and at the ripe old age of seventy-four, and ripe in character, ripe in the affection and esteem of all good men, and ripe in good works, he was gathered to his fathers.

> " Our hearts, though stout and brave,
> Still like muffled drums are beating
> Funeral marches to the grave."

Every heart-beat and we have left one heart-beat less, every heart-beat and we are one heart-beat nearer to the silent land. We are born into this world without our consent. We die without our consent. We glide on in the great tide of humanity, slowly and certainly, as the glacier glides down the mountain side to the sea.

> " For we are the same our fathers have been,
> We see the same sights our fathers have seen,
> We drink the same stream, we view the same sun,
> And we run the same course our fathers have run.
>
> The thoughts we are thinking our fathers did think,
> From the death we are shrinking our fathers did shrink;
> To the life we are clinging they also did cling,
> But it speeds from us all like a bird on the wing."

JUDGE GRESHAM said in response:

Mr. Swett's remarks have recalled to my mind the peculiarly sad and distressing circumstances under which I made the acquaintance of Judge Dickey, then Colonel of the Sixth Illinois Cavalry. I commanded the post at Savannah during the battle of Shiloh, and for a short time thereafter. This place is seven miles below Pittsburg Landing. A large number of wounded men were sent down to us, many coming on Sunday, the first day of the battle; and the stragglers from the battle-field were numerous. Besides this, as General Buell's command was sent forward from this point by steamers, detachments and the stragglers from his army were also to be dealt with and cared for. No preparation had been made, even for the accommodation of the wounded. In this state of confusion, Judge Dickey arrived a day or two after the battle, perhaps the next day, bringing with him General Wallace, who had been wounded, as described by Mr. Swett. With Judge Dickey and General Wallace also came Mrs. Wallace, who was Judge Dickey's daughter, Colonel Ransom, who had also been slightly wounded; and, as I recollect, Major M. R. M. Wallace, a brother of General Wallace. The best that I could do in the way of accommodations for General Wallace was to offer those having him in charge the only room which I then occupied for the transaction of business. General Wallace lingered in great agony until the latter part of the week, as I recollect, when he died.

I shall not undertake to describe that death scene; I

remember, however, with what self-possession, fortitude and courage Mrs. Wallace sustained herself until life in her husband was extinct. Although Mr. Swett has said much in praise of General Wallace, and of the brilliant future which awaited him, he has not spoken extravagantly. Captain Cyrus Dickey, one of Judge Dickey's sons, was on General Ransom's staff in 1863 at Natchez, Mississippi. When General Ransom left there for a short rest, I relieved him, and not caring to go home with his chief, Captain Dickey remained with me as a member of my official family for the time being. He was bright, alert, genial, companionable and resolute. When General Ransom returned, he joined the Red River expedition, Captain Dickey going with him; and in one of the battles of that campaign Captain Dickey was killed.

Naturally enough these circumstances led to an intimate acquaintance and a strong friendship between Judge Dickey and myself. He was no ordinary man. He was patriotic to an extraordinary degree, and felt a profound concern in the fate of his country and its welfare. He was always a just, manly man; he respected himself while he respected the rights of others. It goes without saying, that he was one of the ornaments of his profession in Illinois. As a judge he will rank among the very best that have adorned the bench of this great and still growing state.

The memorial presented by Mr. Swett will be spread upon the records of this court as an enduring testimony of the esteem and regard in which Judge Dickey was held by his professional brethren.

www.ingramcontent.com/pod-product-compliance
Lightning Source LLC
Chambersburg PA
CBHW020707260626
47157CB00008B/3174